A Topps® LEAGUE Story

YOU'RE OUT!

· BOOK FIVE ·

By **Kurtis Scaletta**

Illustrated by **Ethe**

Amulet Bo
New York

D1042821

For Byron, who is more fun than a Whipper Whirl
—K.S.

For Shel
—E.B.

Library of Congress Cataloging-in-Publication Data

Scaletta, Kurtis.
You're out! / by Kurtis Scaletta ; illustrated by Ethen Beavers.
    pages cm. — (A Topps league story ; book 5)
Summary: "Umpire Solomon Johnson throws out the Pine City Porcupines manager, 'Grumps' Humboldt, for arguing a call. Batboy Chad tries to make peace by giving Solomon a rarely issued 'umpire card,' but the ump blows his top. He thinks Chad is making fun of his weight. It's going to be a long nine innings."— Provided by publisher.
    ISBN 978-1-4197-0659-2 (alk. paper)
[1. Baseball—Fiction. 2. Baseball umpires—Fiction. 3. Batboys—Fiction.
4. Baseball cards—Fiction.] I. Beavers, Ethen, illustrator. II. Title. III.
        Title: You are out!
        PZ7.S27912Yo 2013
        [Fic]—dc23
        2012044081

Book design by Chad W. Beckerman

Printed and bound in U.S.A.
10 9 8 7 6 5 4 3 2 1

ABRAMS
THE ART OF BOOKS SINCE 1949
115 West 18th Street
New York, NY 10011
www.abramsbooks.com

CHECKLIST

- [ ] #1 JINXED!
- [ ] #2 STEAL THAT BASE!
- [ ] #3 ZIP IT!
- [ ] #4 THE 823RD HIT
- [ ] #5 YOU'RE OUT!
- [ ] #6 BATTER UP!

hree hundred and fifty-six days out of the year, there's no place I'd rather be than at a baseball game. That's why I'm really lucky to work as a batboy for a minor league team. It was my second season with the Pine City Porcupines, and it's the best job a kid can have.

The other nine days a year there is one place, and *only* one place, that I would rather be: the state fair.

A baseball game can go back and forth, up and down. The state fair has the Whipper

Whirl, a ride that whips you one way and whirls you the other, at five hundred miles an hour.

Baseball has corn dogs and waffle fries and cotton candy and soda pop. The state fair has all of that *plus* cheeseburger wontons, deep-fried pickles on a stick, bacon-butterscotch mini-doughnuts, and a thousand other things you didn't know even existed until you saw them at the fair.

Baseball has the crowd singing "Take Me Out to the Ball Game" in the middle of the seventh inning. The state fair has a parade every morning, right after the gates open, with a marching band and a long line of convertibles, old trucks, and horse and buggies.

Don't get me wrong. Baseball is still my favorite thing in the world, almost all of the time. But baseball goes for the entire summer. The state fair only lasts nine days.

And this year, I was going to miss all nine of them. We were spending a few days at Grandma's, and when we got back, I had to work for the Porcupines.

• • •

On the first day of the state fair, I was on an airplane to Arizona with my mom and dad. We were flying to Tucson to visit my grandmother.

"Why don't we go see Grandma at *Christmas*?" I asked.

"Because she'll be coming to visit in December," said Dad. "She wants a white Christmas, and it rarely snows in Tucson."

"So why did she move there if she wanted snow?"

"Because she was sick of cold weather," Dad explained.

"Hmm." It sounded to me like Grandma wanted to have it both ways.

"Aren't you excited about seeing your grandmother?" Mom asked.

"Sure, but we're missing the state fair," I said.

"You'll still have fun," said Dad. "Grandma's having a party!"

• • •

She did have a party. Grandma's friends were nice, but they were old. They talked about gardens and golf and grandchildren. It was so hot outside that we stayed cooped up inside with the air-conditioning on full blast. I got cold and had to put on a sweater. I hadn't packed a sweater, so I had to wear one of *Grandma's* sweaters. It was pink and said "Life Begins at Sixty." Instead of normal party games, Grandma and her friends tried to teach me whist. The cake had *carrots* in it. I wish I were kidding!

Grandma's next-door neighbor was named Hal. He was even older than Grandma.

"So, I hear you collect baseball cards," Hal said.

"Yeah! I have thousands of cards," I told him. I didn't tell him the cards were magic. The Pine City Porcupines think they are, anyway. Players have done amazing things when they have the right card from my collection. Our jinxed shortstop turned a triple play all by himself. The slowest player on the team stole second base. I think the cards just remind them that in baseball anything is possible.

"As it happens, I have a card in need of a collection," Hal said. He took one out of his breast pocket and handed it to me.

It was a card for an umpire named Eric Gregg. It was signed and everything.

"Thanks," I said. "I know I don't have this

one. How did you get it?" It was a weird card to have if you only had one baseball card.

"I coached Eric as a kid back in Philly," Hal replied. "He sure loved to play, and he ended up being an umpire. Anyway, he visited me once and gave me this card."

"Wow. Why don't you want to keep it?"

"I want to give it to someone who will take good care of it," said Hal. "When your grandmother told me about your collection, I knew you should have it."

It was a neat card.

If umpires could have cards, maybe one day a batboy could have one.

• • •

The first thing I did when I got back home was go to Dylan's house. He's the other batboy for the Pines, and he took care of our dog while we were gone.

"It was fun having Penny here," he told me. "I'm going to miss her." Penny nuzzled Dylan's hand and licked his palm. She barely noticed I was there. Dylan loved animals, and they loved him.

"How was the fair?" I asked him. "Did you see all the animals?" I figured that would have been his favorite part. The fair has buildings full of cows, sheep, pigs, chickens, and rabbits. They even have ostriches and llamas.

"I sure did," said Dylan. "The best part was this horse named Einstein II. He played tic-tac-toe, and bowled, and counted to ten. He must be the world's smartest horse."

"You're not getting a horse!" Dylan's mother hollered from inside the house.

"I know!" he called back. "I never said I wanted a horse," Dylan said to me, "but I guess I've been talking a lot about Einstein II."

"You still have three rabbits," I reminded him.

"Rabbits don't do tricks. At least, mine don't." Dylan shrugged. "Oh, well. See you at work."

I walked Penny home through the park. She loves the park, because there's so much to sniff and bark at.

I ran into two friends from school, Oscar and Ivan.

"How many times did *you* go on the Whipper Whirl?" Oscar asked Ivan.

"Ten times," Ivan answered.

"Well, I went on it *eleven* times," said Oscar.

"I meant, twelve times," said Ivan. "Hey, Chad. How many times did *you* go on the Whipper Whirl?"

"None. I haven't been to the fair this year."

"Wow," said Oscar. "You really need to go and ride the Whipper Whirl."

"Oh, oh, oh! And you have to try the strawberry-rhubarb French toast sundae," said Ivan.

"With marshmallows and chocolate chips," added Oscar.

"And whipped cream," said Ivan.

"And real maple syrup!" they shouted together.

"It's the most amazing thing in the history of food," said Ivan. "I ate two of them."

"I had three," said Oscar.

"That sounds really good," I told them, "but there are Porcupine games every day until the fair is over. I have to work." The fair was in a town that was ninety minutes away by car, so there wouldn't be time to get there and back before Friday's night game. Besides, I'd be way too tired to work.

"Too bad," said Oscar. "I'm going back on Saturday. I'm going to ride on the Whipper Whirl fifteen times and eat four strawberry-rhubarb French toast sundaes."

"I'm going to ride on the Whipper Whirl *twenty* times and eat *five* sundaes," said Ivan.

"Have fun," I told them, but I was jealous. I would have settled for one ride and one sundae.

I stopped by the Speed Pitch booth on my way into the ballpark.

"Hi, Chad," said Kevin, the teenager who worked at the booth. He handed me a baseball. "Think you'll hit thirty miles today?"

"I don't know." I chucked the ball as hard as I could. I saw the score and sighed. Twenty-four miles per hour. Not even close.

"That's really good for a kid your age," Kevin told me.

"Sure it is." I knew that other kids my age can throw twice that fast.

"Hey, you're throwing five or six miles faster than you were a few weeks ago," he said. That was true.

"Nate Link showed me how to throw sidearm," I told him. Nate Link was a relief pitcher for the Porcupines. For some reason, I found throwing sidearm easier. Even Nate was impressed. "Some guys are just sidewinders," he told me.

"Try another one." Kevin passed me the ball. I threw it as hard as I could. Twenty-four . . . again!

"You're throwing straighter," said Kevin. "I bet if you went to the fair, you could clean up at the Pitch-and-Win."

"Not this year," I told him.

I took another ball and pretended there were pins stacked up in a pyramid. I hurled the ball. In my mind, the pins flew everywhere and I won a big stuffed panda.

"Twenty-five!" said Kevin. He slapped my hand. "You're almost there. Try one more?"

"Nah, I'd better go. See you tomorrow."

I walked to the Pines' locker room, still thinking about the state fair. Besides missing out on rides and food, I was missing out on winning stuff!

"What's wrong, kid?" asked Mike Stammer, the shortstop. "Your face is longer than a Sammy Solaris home run."

"Heck, it's longer than Sammy's belt," added Wayne Zane, the catcher. He patted his stomach just in case we didn't get the joke.

"It's longer than the row of candles on Wayne's last birthday cake," Sammy fired back.

"So what's got you down?" Teddy Larrabee asked me. "The Bear" was the first baseman. "I mean, besides their jokes?"

"Just that I won't get to go to the state fair this year."

"That's no fair," said Wayne. "Why, it's no fair at all."

I glared at him.

"Just sayin'," said Wayne.

"What's all this sitting around and yammering?" Grumps Humboldt bellowed. His real name was Harry, but everybody called him Grumps. He was the Porcupines' manager.

"It's time for batting practice," said Grumps. "None of you is hitting good enough to skip batting practice."

"Hey," said Wayne. "We've been hitting pretty well."

"Not well enough. And you'd better get ready for some crazy calls," Grumps said. "Solomon Johnson is umpiring all weekend."

"Uh-oh," said Wayne.

"That's right—Solly himself," said Grumps. "The worst umpire in the Prairie League!" He headed out to the dugout.

"It's going to be a long weekend," said Wayne.

Sammy nodded.

"*¿Por qué?*" asked Diego Prado. He was a new player who mostly sat on the bench. He understood English but spoke in Spanish.

"Grumps will argue every call, that's *por qué*," said Wayne. "At least until he's thrown out."

Diego nodded.

"Solly has thrown him out of more ball games than any other umpire," Sammy added.

Now, that was saying something. Grumps had been thrown out of a lot of ball games. Sometimes, when a manager argues too much or goes too far with an umpire, the umpire ejects him from the game. It means the manager has to leave the field *and* the dugout and can't even talk to the players until the game is over.

Grumps was back in the doorway. He glared at everybody.

"Practice . . . *now*!" he shouted. The players grabbed their bats and gloves and hurried out.

• • •

It was my turn to help the visiting team. After running down fly balls during batting practice, I walked across the field to the other dugout. The Pines were playing the Centralville Cougars. The Cougars were scuffling, which is a baseball term for losing practically every game. This would be a good chance for the Porcupines to pick up a game or two on the Rosedale Rogues, who were leading the Prairie League, as always.

"Hey, Cougars!" a familiar voice shouted. "Why is your town called Centralville? Because it's in the middle of *nowhere*?" It was Ernie Hecker.

Ernie had the biggest mouth in Pine City.

He always sat behind the visiting team's dugout and shouted at the players.

"I don't know why he has to make fun of Centralville," one of the Cougars said. He was really young. If he didn't know about Ernie, he must have just been called up from the Rookie League.

"Don't take it personally, Tim," said the catcher.

Ernie shouted again: "Maybe it should be called Last-Place-Ville!"

"Now, that's hitting below the belt," said Tim.

"Oh, just ignore him," said the catcher.

That was easier said than done. I knew that from experience.

Fortunately, the voice of Victor Snapp, the announcer, drowned out Ernie. Victor Snapp is my hero. I want to be a baseball announcer when

I grow up. "Tomorrow is a big doubleheader," Victor said. "Two games for the price of one, and two-for-one hot dogs all day long. Plus, special musical guests in between games! It'll be a fine way to spend the day if you can't go to the fair."

Even my role model had to remind me I was missing the fair!

• • •

Ernie got going again once the game started. "I've seen a better swing made out of a rope and tire!" he yelled as the first Cougar batter grounded out.

"Thanks for cooling off the ball," he yelled as the second batter went down on strikes.

Tim was the third one up in the inning.

"Ladies and gentlemen, there's a lost toddler on the field!" Ernie yelled. "Are this little boy's mommy and daddy here?"

Tim turned bright red. He went into his stance, but you could tell he was distracted by Ernie's taunts.

Kip Kilgore threw the ball. Tim swung and connected, dropped the bat, and started running. The ball sailed down the left field line and landed very close to the foul line. The umpire signaled that it was a fair ball. Danny O'Brien, the Pines' left fielder, ran after it as Tim rounded first and headed for second.

Grumps came storming out of the dugout.

"What game are you watching?" he shouted. "That ball was so foul it laid an egg!" He went on for several minutes, pushing closer and closer to the umpire.

Solomon Johnson was as tall and wide as the outfield wall. Grumps barely came up to his nose, even when standing on tiptoe. The umpire's face was calm, even though Grumps was shouting.

"That umpire is hard to rattle," said one of the Cougars.

"He sure is," said another. "That's why they call him 'Solly the Snowman.' Because he's so cool."

"Or maybe it's because he's so round," said a fellow Cougar.

Grumps went on shouting. He jumped up and down. He threw his hat. He punched his fist into the air. Solomon Johnson didn't even flinch.

"You tell him, Grumps!" Ernie shouted.

The Porcupines' manager kicked some dirt and stamped his foot and then finally headed back toward the dugout. Before he reached the dugout, he turned back for one last jab: "Go back to umpire school!"

Solomon didn't say a word. He just gestured with his thumb, making an out sign over his shoulder, which meant he was throwing Grumps out of the game.

Grumps was ejected before the Porcupines had even come up to bat! He stormed off the field, passed through the dugout, and headed toward the locker room.

The Porcupines lost the game, 3–2. They slid a game back in the standings. By the time I got to the locker room, the players had showered and dressed, but a few of them were still hanging around, talking about the game.

"We just couldn't come up with the big hit we needed in the eighth," said Tommy Harris, the third baseman, who'd grounded into a double play to end the inning.

"Or the big pitch we needed in the ninth," said Nate Link, who'd given up the winning run.

"Rubbish!" Grumps snorted. "We couldn't make up for all the bad calls."

"Sorry for asking, Mr. Humboldt," said Tommy, "but you didn't see any plays after you were ejected, so how do you know if there were bad calls?"

"Because I know Solomon Johnson was the umpire!" Grumps said. "He has it in for me."

"Sure," said Wayne. "Sure. He has it in for you." He picked up his bag and headed for the door.

"Stop right there," said Grumps.

"What's wrong?"

"That last comment wasn't a wisecrack. What's wrong with you? Are you feeling sick?"

"I'm fine," said Wayne. "I just agreed with you. Solly has it in for you. Nothing you can do. The deck is stacked."

Grumps scowled at Wayne. "Something tells me you don't really think so."

"Look, every time Johnson umpires, you blow up at him," said Wayne. "Maybe *that's* why he has it in for you."

"I blow up only because he always makes bad calls!"

"It's his job to make calls," said Wayne. "Maybe they aren't all the right calls, but I'm sure he's trying."

"Well, it's my job to stick up for my players," said Grumps.

"It's also your job to stay in the game," said Wayne.

"We need you out there, Mr. Humboldt," said Tommy. "You know the game better than any of us. You know when to steal and when to stay on the base."

"Or when to lay down a bunt, and when to swing away," added Sammy.

"Or which pitcher to bring in," said Nate.

"Maybe we would've won the game if you had been there."

"Hmmph." Grumps rubbed his jaw and thought for a moment. "Maybe you guys got a point."

"Tell you what," said Wayne. "How about a friendly wager? I'll bet you can't get through both games of the doubleheader tomorrow without getting booted."

"How much?"

"We won't bet for money," said Wayne. "But the Pine City girls softball league is having a carnival next week, and they need a local celebrity for the dunking both. It's an off day for us, so you'd be perfect."

"So they get to drop me in the drink," said Grumps. He thought it over. "All right, but here's what I want from you guys. My granddaughter is turning six on Sunday, and

I'm having a big party for her after the game. She wants a cowboy, a clown, a superhero, and a magician at her party."

"Wow—all those entertainers will cost a lot," said Wayne.

"Nope," said Grumps. "Pine City doesn't have any of them for hire. But what it does have is a costume store. I'll pay the rentals, and you guys will be the cowboy, the clown, the superhero, and the magician."

"I suppose I can learn a few magic tricks," said Wayne. He turned back to Sammy and Nate. "Who wants to be the clown?"

"Ha!" said Grumps. "Wayne, all you need is a big red nose. You were born to be the clown."

"I'll be the superhero," said Sammy, flexing his biceps.

"Better make sure they have that costume in extra-extra-extra-extra large," said Wayne.

"I'll be the magician," said Nate. "I know a few tricks."

"Well, you sure made that one-run lead disappear," said Wayne.

Nate rolled his eyes.

"Just sayin'," said Wayne.

"I guess that makes me the cowboy," said Tommy. "My family has a few cows back home, so it makes sense."

"It sounds like we have ourselves a wager," said Grumps.

"*Both* ends of the doubleheader," Wayne reminded him. "You have to get through the whole day without getting ejected."

"I know," said Grumps. "You guys better start practicing your lassos and card tricks and feats of strength. And Wayne?"

"Yeah?"

"You don't need to change a thing."

• • •

"Any closer to getting a horse?" I asked Dylan on the way across the parking lot. He walked with his bike so he could talk to me.

"No way," he said. "I looked it up on the Internet. Horses cost a lot. Plus you have to keep them at a stable, and *that's* expensive.

"I'll come over and help you build a horse house!" I said. "We have plans for a doghouse. We just need to multiply everything by ten."

"Ha. I don't think that'll work," Dylan replied.

"Hmm. Well, Penny just sleeps at the foot of the bed, anyway. How big is your bed?"

"Not big enough."

I snapped my fingers. "Just put it in the hutch with the rabbits!"

"Yeah, you're almost as funny as Wayne Zane," said Dylan. "Hey, see you tomorrow."

"It'll be a long day," I said. "Doubleheader."

"Yep." Dylan got on his bike and pedaled away. When he was about a hundred yards away, I thought I heard him shout "Giddyap!" It could have been my imagination.

I stopped by the Speed Pitch booth again on my way into the ballpark.

"You're going to hit thirty," said Kevin. "I can feel it." He handed me a ball.

I hurled the ball with all my might, this time using my sidearm pitch.

"Twenty-*three*?" My pitches were slowing down.

"You're just getting warmed up," said Kevin. He handed me another ball.

I threw a few more pitches but didn't hit yesterday's speed.

"Just keep practicing," said Kevin.

Dylan passed us on his way to the Pines' locker room.

"Want to give it a go?" Kevin asked.

"Sure."

I figured Dylan would show me up without even trying. He was pretty good in gym class.

Dylan threw the ball. It flopped into the net. Thirteen miles per hour. That was slow. I realized Dylan didn't know *how* to throw. He didn't use a windup at all.

"Want me to show you how?" I asked him.

"Maybe later," Dylan said with a shrug. He didn't care much about sports, not even baseball. Maybe he would take up rodeo or polo—something with horses.

• • •

I changed into my batboy uniform and made coffee.

"Don't forget to make more before the second game," said Lance Pantaño as he filled his mug. "I'm pitching." Lance was in the habit of drinking a few cups of coffee before every game, and baseball players are sticklers for tradition.

"Thanks for the reminder. I'll make some before I leave." I was going to work in the Porcupines' dugout for the first game, then go over to help the Cougars for the second game.

I relaced a few pairs of shoes and set up the bat rack. A delicious smell filled the room as Sammy came in with a tray from the snack bar.

"Do you have *four* corn dogs?" Wayne asked Sammy.

"It's two-for-one today, and I always get two," Sammy explained.

"I thought you were trying to keep it to one," said Tommy.

"But today's a doubleheader." Sammy dipped one of his corn dogs in mustard and took a bite.

"Does that mean you'll have four more before the second game?" asked Tommy.

Sammy's eyes got wide as he thought it over. "Good point. Here, you'd better take one."

Tommy did, and so did Wayne.

Lance just scowled. "I don't eat junk food," he said.

"Chad?" Sammy offered me the last dog.

I took it. "Thanks!"

"It was two-for-one," Sammy said. "It was nothing."

"Food is always free for players anyway," I reminded him.

"But it was two-for-one!"

Who was I to argue? It was a corn dog.

Besides, today was a doubleheader. I needed to fuel up.

• • •

I went out for batting practice. Dylan and I helped field all the fly balls the hitters sent into the outfield.

"Does something seem weird to you?" asked Dylan. I looked around.

"More kids than usual?"

"More *girls* than usual," he said.

He was right. There *were* a lot of girls in the stands.

"Is there some kind of promotion today?" he asked. "Girls get in free?"

"I don't think so," I told him. "Girls like baseball. That's all."

A ball came my way. I fielded it and threw it toward the bull pen. The ball felt fast coming out of my hand—maybe even thirty miles an

hour. I made a game of it all through batting practice for both teams, throwing the ball as hard as I could. By that time, Pokey the Porcupine mascot and Spike the junior mascot were circling the field. The crowd cheered as the mascots threw T-shirts and caps into the stands.

Spike waved at me as they passed.

"Hi, Abby!" I whispered. That was the name of the kid in the costume. She was a friend of mine from school.

"Hey, Chad!" she whispered back. She wasn't supposed to talk when she was in costume, but nobody could hear her over the noise. "Can I ask you for a huge, tremendous, really important favor?"

"Sure. Shoot."

Before she could ask, Grumps appeared.

"Hey, you. Batboy. Get in here!"

I gulped. Grumps almost never talked directly to me, and when he did, it was never good.

"Sorry, I'll have to talk to you later," I told Abby. I ran to the dugout.

"You set up the bats for the second game!" said Grumps.

I looked and saw he was right. First, I had Wayne's bats in the rack. Wayne couldn't catch two games in a row. It was too hard on his knees. So the backup catcher, Benito Oseguedo, would catch the first game. I also had Diego Prado's bats in the rack. Diego was going to play left field for the *second* game, but Danny O'Brien was playing the first game.

"I'll fix it," I said.

"Be quick about it," said Grumps. "The game starts in a few minutes."

I got back to the dugout just in time for the

national anthem and the ceremonial first pitch. Then the Centralville Cougars came up to bat. The first batter drew a walk. So did the second batter.

Grumps fumed. "I don't know where the strike zone is, but I know it's not wide enough to let in a baseball."

It's against the rules to argue about strikes and balls with the umpire, so Grumps had to keep his opinion to himself. He'd get ejected in a second if he said anything.

As the inning wore on, Grumps got huffier and puffier, until he could have blown down the entire ballpark with a single snort.

The next batter up got a base hit, and the runner on second rounded third and headed home. Mike threw the ball to Benito, who tagged the runner out.

At least that's what it looked like.

Solomon Johnson signaled that the runner was safe.

"What?"

Managers *are* allowed to argue about runners being safe or out. Grumps stormed out of the dugout.

"Remember the bet!" Sammy shouted. "You can't get ejected."

"Hmm. Maybe you're right. Better not risk it." Grumps came back and sat on the bench, still glaring at the umpire and grumbling to himself.

Finally the inning was done, and the Cougars had scored only one run. I went to get Tommy's bat. He was the first hitter for the Pines. I also grabbed the bat for Myung Young, the Pines' center fielder. He was batting second.

"We'd better get the same strike zone," Grumps was saying when I got back.

No such luck. Tommy took a pitch that was way high, but it was called a strike. He fouled off a pitch, then took another high pitch for a strike. He was out.

"Gabbagah!" Grumps shouted. He rubbed his face in disbelief. "Worse thing is, I can't say a word. Nope, I just have to sit here and take it."

"That's right," said Wayne. "Unless you want to go give him a piece of your mind. Tell him to go back to umpire school."

"You're egging me on," said Grumps. "I know your scheme. You want me to get kicked out so I can let those kids at the carnival beat me up like a piñata."

"It's just a dunk tank," said Wayne. "It's like going swimming."

"I don't know how to swim."

"So it'll be the perfect chance to learn," said Wayne.

"No, sir," said Grumps. "I'm staying right here. You practice your clowning." He leaned over and patted Wayne's knee. "As if you need any practice."

By the fifth inning, I was sure Grumps was going to explode. You could practically see the steam puffing out of his ears.

I had an idea. Maybe one of my baseball cards could help Grumps keep cool and stay in the game. I had only a few manager cards in the binder, but one of them might work.

The Porcupines were out in the field, so I had a few seconds to slip into the locker room and take a look at my red baseball-card binder.

Did Joe Torre ever yell at umpires? I wondered. Or how about Jim Leyland?

"Hey, Kid Magic," said Wayne, using my clubhouse nickname. "Looking for a card to save the day?" He must have seen me sneak back there.

"Just trying to help Grumps," I said.

"Let me see," he said. He flipped through the pages of cards in plastic sleeves. "How about this one?" He pointed at one of my uncle Rick's cards. "He was a real sweet guy. Everybody called him 'Billy Smiles,' because he always had one on his face."

"Really?"

"He was truly the salt of the earth," said Wayne. "Nicest guy to ever play the game or manage a team. The problem is, Grumps doesn't believe in magic. If you want the card to work, you'll just have to plant it on him. Maybe slide it into his pocket when he's not paying attention."

"I don't know about that," I admitted. "I

think a card works only if the player believes in it, and Grumps can't believe in it if he doesn't even know about it."

"Give it a try," said Wayne. "Slip that card to him. I bet Grumps gets chillier than a cucumber milk shake."

"OK . . . I guess it won't hurt to try." I put the Billy Smiles card in my pocket and followed Wayne back to the dugout.

Planting the card was way easier said than done, I realized. Grumps was pacing, fuming, and grumbling. There was no way to shove something in his pocket without him noticing.

The top of the inning was over, and the Porcupines ran off the field. I saw something at the end of the bench—the clipboard! Grumps kept score for every game, and he kept his scorecards on a clipboard.

When Grumps had his back turned, I undid the clasp on the clipboard, slid my baseball card

under all of the sheets, and clamped it down
again. There was no way he'd know the card
was there.

"What are you doing?" Grumps growled.

"Uh—I was just looking at your scorecard,"
I said. "What does BC stand for?" I'd never seen
that before.

"Blown call," Grumps muttered. "There've been at least six so far."

"Got it."

"But leave my stuff alone," he said. "Don't let me catch you tampering with it again."

"Yes, sir."

"Good save," Wayne whispered.

I hoped that the magic would work even if Grumps didn't know that Billy Smiles was back there, helping him calm down and stay in the game.

• • •

Benito, the backup catcher, was the first to bat for the Pines the next inning. Grumps went back to snorting about the size of the strike zone while Benny took a pitch for a strike, swung through the second, and held up on the third. Solomon Johnson ruled that it was a strike-out.

"That wasn't a swing, and it sure wasn't over the plate," Grumps fumed. He made the BC mark on his card, using so much force that he broke his pencil lead. Apparently, the magic card wasn't working.

"I'll sharpen that for you," I offered.

"You worry about the bats," said Grumps. "I have another pencil right here." He parked the broken pencil behind his ear and took another one from behind his other ear.

I put Benny's bat away and got Tommy's so he could take practice swings on deck.

Danny O'Brien was batting. He hit a fly ball that was caught. Grumps muttered, even though there was no way for an umpire to get *that* wrong.

Diego Prado nudged me. *"El puercoespín es aquí,"* he said, pointing at Spike.

"The porcupine is here? Oh, gotcha!!" I

moved closer so Abby could talk to me. "What's up? You said something about a favor?"

"Yes. The Blue Yodels are playing between games," she whispered.

"Who?"

"They're a musical group," she explained. "I just saw them at the fair. They're amazing!"

"If you say so." To me, they sounded like a bunch of old codgers.

"Anyway, I really want Shane's autograph, but I can't talk while I'm in costume."

"Who's Shane?"

"One of the singers in the Blue Yodels. I heard that they're already here, but I don't know where. Oh, rats, I don't have pen or paper."

"No problem. We have plenty. How do I know which one is Shane?"

"He's the lead singer. Thanks, Chad! You're my hero!" She slapped a porcupine paw against my hand and ran away from the dugout.

rumps was still upset with practically every call the umpire made. He cussed and complained and clomped around. He turned eight shades of red and six shades of purple and one color I'd never seen before. The only reason he was still in the game was that he hadn't actually yelled at the umpire yet. He yelled at everybody in the dugout instead.

"Stop snapping your gum!" he barked at Luis Quezada, one of the bench players.

"Keep your feet off the railing," he said, glaring at Wayne.

The card obviously wasn't working. I was sure someone named Billy Smiles wouldn't talk to his players like that.

The Cougars were ahead, 2–0, but it could have been a lot worse. Then one of the Cougars got on base with two outs in the top of the seventh.

Kyle Kostelnik was pitching for the Porcupines. He threw to first base to keep the runner from taking a big lead. Teddy threw it back. Kyle looked like he might pitch to the batter, and the runner took a big lead. Kyle quickly threw to first again.

He picked off the runner! Three outs! The crowd went crazy.

But Solomon Johnson pointed at Kyle, and then he pointed at the runner, and then he pointed at second base.

"He's saying it was a balk," Sammy explained.

A balk is when a pitcher goes too far in trying to fake out the runner. It meant the runner was not only NOT out, he got to take an extra base.

"That's it!" Grumps stalked out of the dugout and headed for the umpire.

"He's done for," said Wayne.

As he neared the umpire, Grumps started shouting. He pointed at the runner, then at Kyle, and then he pointed at his feet.

Solomon Johnson had the same expression he always did, which was none at all. He just stood there, not even blinking, while Grumps yelled and hollered. And when Grumps was done, Solomon Johnson hooked his thumb over his shoulder.

Grumps was out of the game!

The Pines' manager stomped back to the dugout.

"You win," he snorted at Wayne. "I had to say *something*." Grumps went into the locker room. An ejected manager couldn't stay in the dugout.

Kyle got the next Cougar out, at least, so the balk didn't hurt him.

• • •

Victor Snapp's voice rang out over the PA system. "As you know, the hit musical group the Blue Yodels will be performing between games today. And as a sneak preview, here they are now to lead us in 'Take Me Out to the Ball Game.'"

There was a lot of shrieking and clapping from the stands. The Blue Yodels must have had a lot of fans at the game.

This was my chance to get an autograph for Abby! I ran into the clubhouse and looked for paper. Grumps was there, pacing between the rows of lockers and muttering to himself. He didn't even notice me. I got a piece of paper and a pen from the shelf by the bat rack and slipped out.

When I got back, I saw that I was completely wrong about the Blue Yodels. They weren't old codgers. They were teenage boys with big shiny smiles and bangs hanging down in their faces. Now I knew why there were so many girls at the game!

The band finished up the song. ". . . at the old . . . ball . . . game!"

"Once again, the Blue Yodels!" Victor Snapp told the crowd. You could barely hear him over all the screaming girls. The group crossed the field and disappeared into the door next to the visitor's dugout. I didn't get a chance to ask for an autograph.

I went back to the locker room to fetch

Sammy's bat. He'd be the first one up in the bottom of the inning.

Grumps was rummaging through the shelf. "Now where did it go?" he complained. "Had it right here."

I flipped the paper in my hand and saw a list of Cougar pitchers and their stats.

"Looking for this?" I asked meekly.

"Yep," he said. "Don't know where you found it, but thanks." Grumps unclamped his clipboard to slide it in, and some of the papers slid to the floor.

"I'll get them," I said. Anything to make him a little less angry. I gathered up the score sheets and stats. When I looked up, Grumps was staring at the clipboard. There was one thing still stuck to it.

"What's this?" he asked, showing me the clipboard.

I gulped. "It's a baseball card."

"I know it's a baseball card. But what's it doing here? Did you put a bugaboo on me?"

"No!"

"They call you Kid Magic," he said. "Don't think I haven't heard. You're some kind of wizard with your cards. And if this isn't a bugaboo, what is it?"

"It's, um . . ." I felt really small. "It was supposed to . . ."

"It's a bugaboo!" He flung the card. It spun and landed on the floor in front of me.

Wally, the clubhouse manager, came over. "What's wrong, Harry?"

Grumps pointed at me. "This batboy gave me a bugaboo!"

"He did what?"

"He gave me a jinxed card!" said Grumps. "He's in cahoots with that rapscallion of a catcher. He got me thrown out of the game."

"Now, Harry. Chad is a good kid, and I don't think he'd do that."

"The proof is right there!" Grumps hollered. "I don't want him sneaking around our locker room anymore."

"You don't mean . . . ," Wally started.

"I want him gone!"

Wally frowned. "Chad, I guess we need to talk."

We went back to the equipment room, which doubled as Wally's office.

"Now, what happened?" he asked.

"I hid a baseball card on Gr—on Mr. Humboldt's clipboard, so he wouldn't get ejected."

"You thought it would be a good-luck charm, eh?"

"Yeah."

Just then Wayne came in. "Er, Wally? I think I can explain."

Wally rubbed his face with his hand. "I should have known *you* were behind this. What did you do?"

"He told me to give Grumps this card," I explained. I gave Wally the card. "I was hoping Billy Smiles would help Grumps keep his cool."

"Billy who?" Wally frowned at the card. "This is Billy *Martin*."

"'Billy Smiles' was his nickname."

"Wayne told you that?"

I nodded.

Wally's mustache twitched, and then he hooted. He chuckled and guffawed. He sniggered and roared. And just when I thought he was done, he was off on another round of laughter.

"'Billy . . . ,'" he said. He had to catch his breath. "'Billy Smiles'!" he laughed some more, slapping his knees. "That's a good one."

"That wasn't his nickname?" I asked.

"Kid," said Wally, "Billy Martin got a lot of teams into the playoffs, but he was as hot-tempered as they come. He sure wasn't famous for smiling."

"Oh, no!" *That's* why Grumps thought I was putting a bugaboo on him.

"Listen, Chad," said Wayne, "I sure didn't mean to get you in trouble. I'll tell Grumps what happened."

"I'll talk to him, too," said Wally.

"OK. Thanks."

"But, uh, not until later," said Wayne. "He's kind of steamed right now."

"Yeah, better to wait until his feathers are unruffled," Wally agreed. "Tell you what, Chad. Just take it easy for the rest of the game. Then you and Dylan swap sides for the second game, and maybe by tomorrow Grumps will have cooled off. And, Wayne, since this is your doing, you be batboy for the rest of the game. You're not in the game, anyway."

"Sure, Wally."

"You'd better stay out of the way," Wally told me. "Lie low. Watch the game from the seats or something."

I felt a pang. I'd have to sit in the stands like a regular fan. I wouldn't be part of the team.

• • •

The game wasn't sold out, so there were empty seats. I wandered up into the left field stands and took the worst one available—top row, and farthest from the action. I brought my binder with me, and put the Billy Martin card back in its slot. I flipped through the pages, remembering the times that one of my baseball cards had saved the day. This was the first time a card had failed me.

Of course, I'd used the worst possible card.

Sammy got a base hit. For most runners, it would have been a double, but since Sammy was slow, it was only a single. Teddy batted next, and he also got a hit. That should have been a double, too, but he was trapped behind Sammy.

Grumps would have put in a pinch runner, I thought. If the Porcupines had replaced Sammy with Luis, he would have scored, and now Teddy would be on second. They would be behind by one run instead of two. Grumps might have a bad temper, but he knew how to win ball games.

"Excuse me."

I looked up and saw a teenager in a denim jacket. His teeth were blinding white. It was one of the Blue Yodels.

"Yeah?"

"My name is Shane," he said. "I saw you before the game. You were catching balls and throwing them again?"

"Yeah. Right. That was me. I'm a batboy."

"That must be a fun job."

"It sure is! Are you a baseball fan?"

"Not really," he admitted. "This is the first time I've ever been to a game."

"Really? Are you from another country?"

He laughed. "No, I'm from New Jersey. I guess I've always been too focused on singing and dancing to watch or play sports."

"At least it paid off," I said. "You're famous now."

"Yeah, but it's also kind of scary. For example, the Porcupines asked me to throw out the first pitch in the second game today."

"That's awesome!" I said. I'd always wanted to throw out a first pitch. "What's scary about that?"

"I don't know how to throw, and I have to do it in front of all these fans. What if I can't get the ball to the catcher?"

"Come on—it's not that hard."

"But I don't want to look like a goof. Can you show me how to throw a baseball?"

I glanced back at the field. George grounded into a double play. Now Sammy was on third base with two outs. It could have been a big inning, but it wasn't.

"Sure," I told him. "I've got nothing better to do."

"I don't want to practice in front of all these people," said Shane.

"I know just the place."

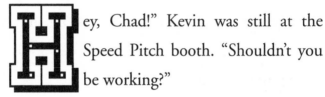ey, Chad!" Kevin was still at the Speed Pitch booth. "Shouldn't you be working?"

"I have a special assignment," I told him. "Shane here is throwing out the first pitch and needs to work on his throw."

Kevin passed him a ball. "Let's see what you can do."

Shane threw an underhand pitch, barely getting the ball to the net. The pitch was so slow the meter didn't even show a number.

"Nice try," said Kevin. "But try throwing it overhand."

"Let me show you," I said, handing Shane my binder. I took a ball, planted my feet, and threw the ball.

The meter flickered: Thirty-one. My best pitch ever!

"Wow," said Shane. "Show me how to do that!"

So I did. Half an hour and fifty pitches later, Shane was throwing straight and fast into the net. His pitches were in the low twenties.

The other Blue Yodels had found us and were cheering him on.

"I think you can throw that first pitch without embarrassing yourself," said Pierce.

"And the rest of us," said Jeff.

"I really owe you one," said Shane to me. "Anything we can do to pay you back?"

"Um . . . just an autograph for my friend Abby."

"No problem," he said.

"Hey, I'll get a group photo from the bus," said Pierce. "We can all sign it."

"Great idea," said Jeff.

"Thanks. She'll love it! Shane, when you're on the field to throw out the first pitch, give the photo to the kid porcupine mascot and say that it's for Abby. Spike will, uh, deliver it to her."

"Sure, no problem. We might even do you one better."

•   •   •

A little while later, I hurried to the Cougars' locker room. Through the dugout door, I could hear the Blue Yodels playing. They were almost drowned out by screaming fans. I stored the binder in an empty locker.

"Hey," said Dylan. "Man, am I glad to see you. Ernie is louder than ever."

"Ugh." I'd forgotten all about Ernie Hecker.

"Better hurry over to the Pines' locker room," I said. "You have to make coffee."

"Why didn't you do it?"

"Long story. I'll explain later. Go make coffee! Lance needs it."

"OK, OK." Dylan started to leave.

I thought of something else. "Don't forget to redo the bats," I said. "And stay out of Grumps's way. He's in a bad mood."

"Got it," Dylan said. "Make coffee . . . redo the bats . . . and stay away from Grumps."

"And most importantly, do not listen to Wayne."

"I know *that*," he said.

I went out to the dugout. The Cougars were watching the band play.

"Know what I love about these guys?" Tim shouted to one of the other players.

"Their harmonies?"

"Nope."

"Their wholesome image?"

"Nope."

"What, then?"

"The noise drowns out that loud guy."

"Yeah. I love that about them too," the other player agreed.

I laughed. Too bad the Blue Yodels couldn't play *during* the second game.

"Our next song is almost a hit," Shane told the crowd. "It's climbing the charts, anyway, and we want to dedicate it to Abby, a friend of Spike the Porcupine and Chad the Batboy." They launched into the song "Hush, Girl." I'd heard it on the radio but didn't know who sang it. Across the field I saw Spike wobble a bit. I hoped Spike . . . er, Abby . . . didn't faint.

"Hey, how did the first game turn out?" I

asked Tim when he got back to the Cougars' dugout.

"We won, four to one, but we got lucky," he said. "The Porcupines nearly blew the game open in the seventh, but their rally fizzled."

"I saw that part, but I missed the rest." If Grumps had still been in the game, the Pines might have won. I hoped he could keep his cool for the second game. The problem was, Solomon Johnson was still going to be there. And since Grumps had already lost his bet with his own team, he wouldn't care if he got ejected.

Then I realized: I was going about this all wrong. Grumps was only half the problem.

The other half of the problem was the umpire, and I had the perfect card for him.

9

The umpires had a room right by the visitors' locker room. I'd never been in there before. Through the door, I could hear loud opera music blaring. I banged on the door. And banged. And banged.

Solomon Johnson finally answered the door. The other umpires were there too, reading.

"Sorry," Johnson said. "We couldn't hear you over the music. Have to drown out that infernal racket from outside."

"They're called the Blue Yodels," I told him.

"More like caterwauling than yodeling,"

Johnson replied. "What do you want? The game doesn't begin for twenty minutes. I need this time to rest."

"I know, I know. I just . . . I feel bad for how our manager hollers at you, so I got a little present for you." I gave him the baseball card.

He took it, stared at it, and frowned. His face reddened. He snorted. "Is this some kind of jest?"

"What?"

"Comparing me to Eric Gregg! Of all the nerve!" Johnson seemed to swell up like a balloon, and then he let me have it. He called me a poorly behaved urchin and a brat. He called me a reprehensible scamp and an inexcusable imp. He called me a lot of things, and I didn't know what they meant, but I didn't need a dictionary to know they weren't any good.

"You're lucky I can't eject batboys from the

game!" he said. Then he slammed the door in my face.

I couldn't believe it. My cards had failed me again. What made "Solly the Snowman" have a meltdown? Was Eric Gregg another "Billy Smiles"? Was he famous for making bad calls? I put the baseball card back in the binder and put the binder in an empty locker. So much for being magic. The only magic they had today was making things worse!

• • •

I returned to the Cougars' dugout just in time to see Shane throw out the first pitch. He threw a strike right over the plate.

"Not bad," said one of the Cougars.

"Betcha that kid played ball," said another player.

"You pitch better than you sing!" Ernie hollered.

I felt good for about ten seconds. Then I saw Solomon Johnson plod out to his spot behind the plate, scowling at the world. He glared in the general direction of the Porcupines' dugout. Grumps stood by the railing and glared back.

Now he's *really* out to get us, I thought.

"It's no use trying to dig your way out of this one," Ernie shouted at the first batter as he stamped down the dirt in the batter's box. "What are you doing, swatting a fly?" he asked as the player swung at the first pitch.

He kept hectoring the batter until he was out.

Tim came to the plate, looking anxious.

"This Cougar is a kitten!" Ernie shouted. "He just got called up from T-ball last week." Tim got flustered and swung weakly at the first pitch. The ball dribbled to first base for an easy out.

"I haven't had a hit since that lucky one yesterday," Tim said when he got back to the dugout. "I can't concentrate with that guy yelling at me."

"You just got to get used to it," said the Cougars' catcher. "There are guys like that in every ballpark."

"Hey," said Tim. "That gives me an idea." He whispered his idea to the catcher. He smiled and whispered it through the dugout.

I wondered what they were up to.

I would have to wait to find out because

the third batter was out. The Cougars took the field.

Tommy batted first for the Pines, and he hit a line drive right over Tim's glove.

"Hey, you need a taller shortstop!" Ernie shouted.

The inning went well for the Porcupines. Myung bunted, sending Tommy to second base, and Mike brought him home with a single. The Porcupines were up by a run! Sammy and Wayne both made outs, but it was nice to have a lead.

"That guy is loud!" said Tim when he was back in the dugout. "I heard him even out on the field."

He talked ten times louder

than he had to, and his voice drifted up into the stands.

"Ah, he's not as bad as Mitch O'Malley in Centralville," said the Cougars' catcher in the same booming voice. "Now, *there's* a guy with a loud voice."

"Yep, Mitch's voice really carries," said a third player, almost shouting. "He sure is hard to ignore."

They paused.

"What are you talking about down there?" Ernie's voice called back.

Tim and the catcher bumped fists. Their plan was working.

The next batter was old for a minor leaguer—not as old as Wayne Zane but older than anyone else on the Cougars.

"Hey, grandpa!" Ernie shouted. "Don't sprain your hip swinging at these fastballs."

"This guy just makes it up as he goes," said Tim, resuming his loud voice.

"Now, Mitch O'Malley—he does his research," said the catcher. "He comes prepared."

"Yep, he really knows how to get under your skin."

The batter beat out an infield hit. He was faster than he looked. The first-base umpire ruled that he was safe. I was surprised Grumps didn't come out to argue about it, but he didn't have a bone to pick with the first-base umpire— just with Solomon Johnson.

The next Cougar batter had long hair sticking out from his batting helmet.

"Hey, Rapunzel!" Ernie called out. "Why don't you let down your hair so the Cougars can *climb* out of last place?"

"That guy's working too hard for laughs," said the Cougars catcher. "Mitch O'Malley—

he's naturally funny. He gets the crowd behind him, and then you're sunk."

"Yeah," another player agreed in a loud voice. "Tim, just wait until you hear Mitch O'Malley. He's a top-notch comedian."

"Ah, can it!" Ernie yelled. "They're ain't no 'Marshmallow' or whatever his name is!"

"Wow," said the catcher. "That's something Mitch never would do."

"Whassat?" asked Tim.

"Let us get to him," he said loudly. "Kind of a rookie move."

And for the first time since I'd become a batboy, Ernie couldn't think of anything to say.

10

I had seen an unassisted triple play and also a perfect game. I had even seen a balloon crash onto the field during a ball game. But the strangest thing I ever saw was what happened in the bottom of the second inning.

Teddy batted first and hit a double. Diego Prado came up next—he was playing left field instead of Danny. Diego got a base hit too, and Teddy came charging home. The Cougar's left fielder got the ball on a bounce and hurled it to the plate.

It was a *really* close play. Solomon Johnson checked to make sure the catcher had the ball and then called Teddy out.

Here we go, I thought.

Sure enough, Grumps rushed out to argue. He stormed across the field toward home plate, and I was sure he would throw his hat, kick dirt, and get himself booted out of the game. But halfway there, he stopped. He scratched his head like he was thinking things over.

Teddy passed him on the way to the dugout. Grumps patted him on the back. "Nice try," he seemed to say. Then he started walking again. He went straight over to Solomon Johnson, so close that he bumped up against Solly's chest protector. Then Grumps stretched out his arms and *hugged* the umpire. He said something. The umpire said something back, and they both burst into tears.

"What's going on?" one of the Cougars asked.

"I don't know for sure," I admitted. "But I think they just made up."

• • •

The Porcupines won, 3–0.

I don't think the Porcupines would have won without Grumps. For example, Grumps saw that the Cougars' second baseman wasn't quite in position, so he signaled for Diego to steal second base. It was risky, but it worked. Diego ended up scoring the second run of the game. Grumps made smart decisions later too. He had Ryan Kimball pitch two innings instead of one, like he usually does, and he put Luis Quezada in as a pinch runner.

I really wanted to know what had happened between Grumps and Solly. It sure looked like Grumps was about to blow up again, but he didn't. Why not? Maybe Dylan could tell me. I couldn't wait to get back to the Pines' dugout and ask.

I was halfway across the infield when I heard a blast of music. Or something *like* music. It was also something *unlike* music and a lot more like noise!

The Porcupines were marching along, humming "Take Me Out to the Ball Game." They weren't in sync or in tune. Dylan led the way, on his bike, popping wheelies. In the back were Pokey and Spike on a golf cart, waving at the empty seats.

They stopped.

"Hey, Chad!" said Abby. "That signed photo is the coolest thing ever, and I *loved* the song. Thanks!"

"You're welcome," I told her.

"So, do you want a ride?"

"It's only like twenty more feet to the locker room."

"But it's a *ride*," she said. "It's not a Whipper Whirl, but it's a ride."

I laughed. "OK. Thanks." I climbed aboard, and Pokey took off at high speed. High speed on a golf cart is not fast at all, but it was fun! Pokey did doughnuts and figure eights and zigzags all over the outfield. When he finally pulled up in front of the Porcupines' dugout, I was dizzy enough to have taken fifteen consecutive rides on the Whipper Whirl.

Before I could even get off the cart, Wally came out, leading Sammy on what looked like a leash. Wayne was behind him, stooped over and holding Sammy's waist.

What the heck?

"This is Newton II, the second smartest horse in the world," Wally explained.

I laughed. Sammy and Wayne were a two-man horse act without a costume.

"You laugh now, but wait until you see this horse," said Wally. "Newton, what's three plus five?"

The horse tapped out seven.

"What's two plus two?"

The horse tapped out seven again.

"Well, he's still smarter than most baseball players," said Wally.

"What else can he do?" I asked.

"He did my taxes," said Wally. "Maybe that's why I got in so much trouble."

The horse neighed and did a little prance, and only broke in half a couple of times.

"That's a great horse," I said. "I think I'll give him to Dylan."

"Nah, I don't think I can teach that horse any tricks," Dylan replied.

"Well, show's over," said Wally. "Thanks to Sammy for playing the front end of the horse, and thanks to Wayne for playing himself."

The guys all had a big laugh while Wayne tried to think of a comeback.

"We felt bad you had to miss the fair," Wally told me. "Your friends here came up with all this." Spike and Dylan each took a little bow. "Besides, your magic kept Grumps in the game."

"I don't know about that," I replied.

Grumps had blown up when he saw the card I gave him, and Solly blew up at the card I gave him. The cards just weren't working that day.

A moment later, Ryan Kimball ran out of the bull pen, carrying a big bowl.

"Special order from the snack bar!" he announced. "Frozen yogurt sundae with strawberry-rhubarb sauce. And they Frenched up a little toast, just for you."

There were no marshmallows or chocolate chips, but it looked delicious. It looked amazing. It also looked like way more than I could eat in a million years.

"I'm going to share it," I said.

"I was hoping you would say that," said Ryan.

"Me too," said Wayne. "But there's probably not enough for everyone, so maybe just you and your favorite horse can split it?"

"Sorry," I said. "I have another idea."

11

I wasn't sure anyone would be in the umpires' room, but on the third knock a voice shouted to come in.

I opened the door slowly. There was classical music playing in the background.

Solomon Johnson was there, in his street clothes, but his shoes were still off. He was blinking like he'd just woken up.

"Dozed off for a bit," he said. "Long day. What you got there?"

"Just wanted to bring a snack." I showed him the sundae.

"You think just because I'm a big guy, all I want is ice cream?"

"It's kind of healthy," I told him. "It's yogurt, not ice cream. And there's fruit in it."

"Well, never mind—that looks really good. Let's dig in."

We passed it back and forth, taking a few bites each turn.

"Thanks for sharing. This is really delicious."

"No problem," I said.

"I've been on a diet," he said. "I've been really good too. I had a salad for lunch, and I'll have another for dinner. I can have a treat once in a while. About once a week."

I nodded as I took a bite. I would ask Mom for something healthy for dinner too.

"You know that card you gave me?" he said.

"Yeah. Eric Gregg."

"I shouldn't have taken it personally. I get a

lot of jokes about my weight. I guess Eric got the same grief."

"Maybe," I said.

"But Eric Gregg was a great umpire. I really respect him, and I should have taken that card as a compliment."

"That's how I meant it," I told him. "Seriously. I didn't even know why you got so mad."

"I made the same mistake everyone else makes. I looked at a heavyset guy, and all I saw was a heavyset guy."

We ate some more of the sundae, but even the two of us couldn't finish it.

• • •

Most of the players were gone when I got back to the Porcupines' dugout. Dylan was in his street clothes but was half asleep on the bench by the lockers.

"Whoa," he murmured. "Good horsey."

I decided not to interrupt his dreams.

"Just the guy I need to see," said Grumps.

I felt a bit of dread. Maybe he was going to fire me over that baseball card.

"Wayne and Wally set me straight," he said. "I know you were just trying to help."

I felt a huge wave of relief. "Thanks."

"I get emotional during games," Grumps

admitted. "You know, Billy Martin was a good manager, and he won a lot of games. But what people remember best was that he was a scrapper. They remember the fights, not the wins. I want people to remember me differently."

"They will," I said.

"Yeah, right! Did you know the guys call me 'Grumps' behind my back?"

"Really?" I pretended I'd never heard it before.

He winked, and I realized he was kidding me. "I thought about that, and I realized that it was time to just tell Solly I was sorry, and move on. Turns out he was just as happy to bury the hatchet. And you know what? I think he umpired fair and square for most of the day."

"Yeah. I think so too. But . . . um . . . sorry about the dunking booth. And your granddaughter's birthday party."

"Ah, water dries off, and it's for a good cause," said Grumps. "And I got everyone I need for that birthday party."

"Really? You got a cowboy and a superhero?"

"*And* a magician *and* a grade A, top-of-the-line clown," said Grumps. "I figured Wayne Zane cheated, so I'm holding him to his end of the bet."

"But who's playing the other parts?"

"Wayne Zane," said Grumps. "He's going to have some uniform changes tomorrow, let me tell you."

For the first time since I'd known him, Grumps cracked a grin.

About the Author

Kurtis Scaletta's previous books include *Mudville*, which *Booklist* called "a gift from the baseball gods" and named one of their 2009 Top 10 Sports Books for Youth. Kurtis lives in Minneapolis with his wife and son and some cats. He roots for the Minnesota Twins and the Saint Paul Saints. Find out more about him at www.kurtisscaletta.com.

About the Artist

Ethen Beavers has illustrated a bunch of comics and children's books, including the bestselling NERDS series by Michael Buckley. He lives in California and likes fishing and his wife. He roots for the San Francisco Giants and loves to watch *The Natural.* You can see more of his drawings online at http://cretineb.deviantart.com.

Come on into the **Reading**  **Clubhouse!**

Check out these other winning titles in the Topps League Story series featuring Chad, Dylan, Spike, and the Pine City Porcupines.

Keep an eye out for the newest
Topps League Story, Book Six: Batter Up!